THE MISADVENTURES OF DOUGAL

'There can be few TV performers who give as much pleasure as Eric Thompson to viewers (or shall we say listeners) of all ages. Long may he and Dougal flourish.'

John Holmstrom in the *New Statesman*

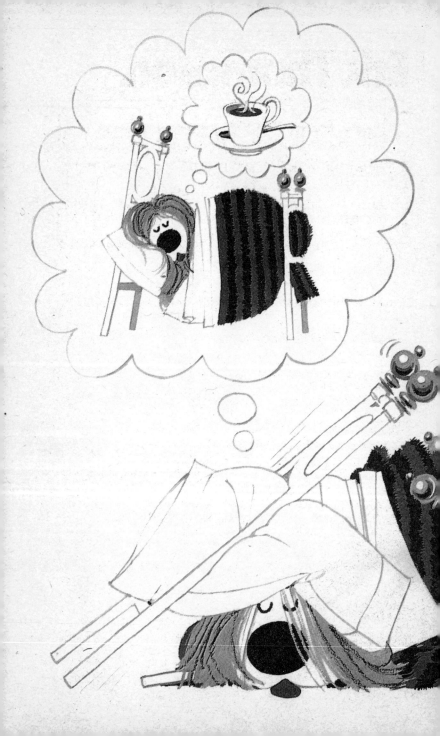

Eric Thompson

The misadventures of

DOUGAL

Based on stories of The Magic Roundabout *by Serge Danot*

Illustrated by David Barnett

KNIGHT BOOKS

in association with SCHOLASTIC PUBLICATIONS

Also available

THE ADVENTURES OF DOUGAL
DOUGAL'S SCOTTISH HOLIDAY
DOUGAL ROUND THE WORLD

ISBN 0 340 16179 5

First published in Great Britain 1972
by Knight Books, the paperback division of
Brockhampton Press Ltd, Leicester

Based on the BBC tv series The Magic Roundabout

Copyright © 1972 Serge Danot

English text copyright © 1972 Eric Thompson
Illustrations copyright © 1972 Brockhampton Press Ltd.
The characters in these stories which appear in the
television films were originally created by
Serge Danot for ORTF in a series entitled
Le Manège Enchanté, and The Magic Roundabout.

Printed and bound in Great Britain by
C. Nicholls & Company Ltd, Manchester

CONTENTS

The Tea Party

Dougal was at home early one morning sipping
a cup of tea and thinking about LIFE. He
finished his tea and thought LIFE was perhaps
a little tedious. He poured himself another cup
and sipped. He brightened.

'Oh, I don't know, perhaps it's not too bad.'

He put down his empty cup.

'Then again,' he thought, 'perhaps it *is*.
Maybe it's something to do with its being
Tuesday. I'm not at my best on a *Tuesday*.
Tuesdays seldom have potential, I find.'

There was a knock at the door.

Dougal got up.

Another knock, louder.

6

'All right, all right, I'm coming,' said Dougal.
A third knock, even louder.
Dougal opened the door.
It was Brian wearing a very large blue cap
and carrying a very large canvas bag.

'Lovely morning, sir,' he said, brightly.
'And what have you come as?' said Dougal.
'What do you mean?' said Brian.
'I mean,' said Dougal, mildly, 'that you are
obviously masquerading as something. I just
wondered what it was, that's all.'
'You're being very mild,' said Brian,
suspiciously. 'Can I come in?'

'I can't think of any reason why you should,' said Dougal.

'Postmen are always asked in,' said Brian, 'and I'm a postman. I bring greetings from afar through hail, snow, sun and mud and I demand to be asked in and provided with comforts.'

'What had you in mind?' said Dougal.

'Well, isn't the kettle on?' said Brian. 'Postmen always get a cup of tea when they've got a letter for someone.'

He pushed past Dougal, went in, sat down and started to whistle a little tune.

Dougal put the kettle on.

'Boiling already?' said Brian.

'Of course not,' said Dougal.

Oh, I thought I heard it whistling,' said Brian.

'That was *you*,' said Dougal.

'Oh,' said Brian.

Dougal made some tea, gave a cup to Brian and sat down.

'Lovely day,' said Brian.

'You've mentioned that,' said Dougal.

'Oh,' said Brian.

He finished his tea.

'Well, I must be off,' he said, getting up.

'Haven't you forgotten something?' said Dougal.

Brian paused.

'No, I don't think so, old chum.'

'Sure?' said Dougal.

'Positive,' said Brian. 'Goodbye.'

He went towards the door.

Dougal stepped on the canvas bag as Brian went by, and Brian somersaulted and landed on his shell upside down, rocking gently.

'You tripped me up,' he squeaked, accusingly.

'An accident,' said Dougal.

'Sure?' said Brian.

'Positive,' said Dougal.

'Oh, that's all right then,' said Brian, rocking.

'Lucky though,' mused Dougal, 'or you might have gone without giving me my letter.'

'Good heavens, so I might,' said Brian, and he tried to right himself.

9

'Having trouble?' said Dougal, rummaging in Brian's canvas bag.

'Hey!' squeaked Brian. 'You're not allowed to do that. Those letters are the property of Her Majesty's Post Office.'

He gave a great heave, righted himself and scuttled into the bag.

'Desist rummaging,' he said, popping his head out.

Dougal pulled at the strap on the bag and lifted it up. Brian disappeared with a thump inside.

'I shall count three,' said Dougal, 'and then if my letter doesn't appear I shall hang this bag on a hook and go on holiday.'

'We postmen aren't easily frightened,' shouted Brian from inside the bag.

'One . . .' said Dougal. 'Two.'
A letter appeared. Dougal dropped the bag.

Brian crawled out.

'I may resign,' he said, slowly.

'Someone, somewhere, needs a letter from you,' said Dougal. 'There's the door – goodbye.'

'I'll report you to the Minister of Posts and Telecommunications,' said Brian.

'Do,' said Dougal.

'He's very fierce,' said Brian.

'Oh, is he?' said Dougal.

Brian went to the door.

'It's an invitation,' he said. 'We've all got one,' and he went out very quickly.

Dougal rushed after him.

'Rotter!' he shouted. 'Spoilsport!'

He jumped up and down with fury.

'Oooh! I hate knowing what's in a letter before I open it. Takes all the fun away. I hope your cap shrinks!' he shouted at Brian.

'See you later!' Brian shouted back.

Dougal sat down to read his letter. It was an invitation from Florence. She'd asked everyone to tea that day and said he was to be sure to come as she'd got everything arranged and lots of lovely things in. 'Just come as you are,' the letter finished.

'Well, I'm not likely to go as anyone else,' giggled Dougal, fiddling around in his drawer for a clean collar.

He brushed his hair and then had a sudden thought.

'I must take her something – a present – some flowers perhaps.'

He hummed a little tune.

'There'll be *cakes*,' he thought, 'so I'll take a lot of flowers.'

Outside the sun was shining and it was very hot. There didn't seem to be many flowers about.

'Someone's been at them,' thought Dougal, darkly. 'I shall go to Mr MacHenry's. He'll have some in his greenhouse.'

But Mr MacHenry hadn't.

'It's this dry weather we've been having,' he said. 'The flowers have withered. We need rain.'

'And I need flowers,' said Dougal. 'Haven't you even got a petunia?'

'Not one,' said Mr MacHenry. 'Need rain, you see, and we won't have rain while the wind is in the South.'

'While the *what* is *where*?' said Dougal.

Mr MacHenry pointed to the weathercock on top of the church.

'See that?' he said. 'Been like that for weeks. Wind's in the South. Needs to be in the West for rain.'

'Oh,' said Dougal, thoughtfully, 'thank you. Er . . . West, you say?'

'West,' said Mr MacHenry, and he went into his greenhouse and started mulching a few things.

Dougal went slowly towards the church. He had to have flowers for Florence – he always took flowers when he went to tea. There seemed to be only one thing to be done. So he did it . . .

Halfway up the church steeple he stopped for breath and looked down.

Everything below seemed very small. He saw Florence's house in the distance, and the Roundabout by Mr Rusty's house was just a speck of colour.

'I hope I'm doing the right thing,' he thought, panting on up.

He passed two pigeons sitting on a ledge.

'Afternoon,' he said.

The pigeons remained silent.

'Suit yourselves,' grunted Dougal, clambering on.

'Was that a dog?' said one of the pigeons.

'Don't be silly, Phyllis,' murmured the other.

Dougal reached the top and paused to get his breath.

He looked at the weathercock. The weathercock looked back at him. It was a tense moment.

'Er . . . I have a request,' said Dougal. 'We need a little rain and you're pointing the wrong way. Might I trouble you to turn to the West?'

'Got any authority?' said the weathercock. 'Letter from the Ministry? Chitty from the Met. Office?'

'Not exactly . . .' began Dougal.

'Can't be done then,' said the weathercock. 'Not without a chitty. In triplicate,' he added.

'I haven't got time to get a chitty,' said Dougal. 'I'm in a hurry.'

'Oh yes, they all say that,' said the weathercock. 'But I don't move a point without a chitty.'

Dougal sighed, eased himself up a little, and slipped.

'Whoops!' he shouted, grabbing the weathercock and spinning around.

'Stop that!' said the weathercock, sharply.

'I can't,' said Dougal, rotating.

'I'm getting dizzy,' shouted the weathercock.

'You're not the only one,' screeched Dougal.

A wind started to blow. The weathercock went round faster and faster.

'You haven't got a chitty!' shouted the weathercock.

'Oh, shut up!' shouted Dougal, trying to find a footing somewhere.

The weathercock bent a little. The wind blew more and more. It started to thunder.

'Oh, I hate it – I hate it!' moaned Dougal.

The weathercock bent a little more. The storm got more and more furious.

Another bend and a squeak, and the weathercock jammed and stopped.

Dougal was thrown off and found himself slithering down the steeple with thunder and lightning crashing all around him. He passed the pigeons very fast.

'I've seen that dog again,' said one.

'I'm getting very worried about you, Phyllis,' said the other.

Dougal reached the bottom just as it started to pour with rain. The weathercock was pointing firmly to the West and Dougal was soaked to the skin.

'Now see what you've done!' shouted the weathercock. 'I'm all bent!'

'I'll let you have a chitty later,' shouted Dougal. And he giggled.

There was a peal of thunder and the rain teemed down. With water dripping off him, Dougal hurried to Mr MacHenry's.

'Lovely weather!' he shouted, through the crashing of thunder. Mr MacHenry didn't answer. He was busy trying to keep the rain out of his greenhouse with a mop.

'Flowers growing?' shouted Dougal.

There was another crash and a wave of water

16

carried Dougal and Mr MacHenry right into the greenhouse.

'The stream's overflowed!' shouted Mr MacHenry, as they sloshed around amongst the flowerpots. 'Everything's ruined!'

They climbed up on to a shelf as the water rose higher.

' Er . . . I thought you needed rain?' said Dougal.

'Rain I needed,' said Mr MacHenry. 'Floods I can do without.'

He grabbed a passing pot of geraniums.

'Look at that! Pitifully bedraggled!'

'Can I have it?' said Dougal.

'Well, I don't want it,' said Mr MacHenry.

Dougal took the pot and looked down. The water seemed very deep and muddy.

'You don't have a boat handy, do you?' he asked.

Mr MacHenry finally snapped.

'No, I do not! This is a nursery, not Portsmouth harbour. Oh dear, oh dear! It'll take me weeks to get this lot right again.'

Dougal decided it was time to leave. He put the pot of geraniums on his head, launched himself into the water and started to swim towards Florence's house.

He met a flock of ducks.

'Lovely weather!' they quacked.

'All right for some!' panted Dougal, battling against the current.

'Did you know you've got a plant pot on your head?' they asked.

'Yes,' gritted Dougal.

He arrived at Florence's. Everyone was there looking out of the window, Mr Rusty, Brian, Ermintrude, Dylan and Zebedee.

'Let me in!' shouted Dougal.

'We can't, the water will come in too!' they shouted back.

'Then open the window!' screeched Dougal.

Florence opened the window and Dougal heaved himself up and fell inside on to the carpet.

18

'I say, you're a bit squelchy,' said Brian.

'You'd be squelchy if you'd been through what I've been through,' said Dougal.

He turned to Florence.

'I've brought you a flower,' he said.

'Oh, Dougal, how lovely,' said Florence. 'You shouldn't have bothered.'

'Oh, it was no bother,' said Dougal. 'Any cake left?'

And there was.

The Roundabout

The next day they discovered a terrible thing.
The great storm had damaged the Magic
Roundabout and Mr Rusty was very upset.
He'd gone to start it up as usual and had found
it all bent and twisted.

'Must have been struck by lightning,' he said,
mournfully. 'I don't like to worry, as you
know, but it's a catastrophe . . . a catastrophe.'

They all walked round looking at the
Roundabout. It was certainly very out of shape.

'Isn't it *awful*, Dougal,' said Florence.

Dougal gulped, feeling very responsible
when he remembered the weathercock.

'Awful,' he squeaked, 'awful.'

'We must do something about it,' said
Florence, firmly.

Everyone agreed that something must be
done about it and they all sat down to think
what to do.

'I know!' said Brian. 'I know! It's simple!
It's so simple I don't know why we didn't think
of it straight away.'

Tell us, Brian,' they said.

'Yes, come on, master mind,' said Dougal.

'The Roundabout is broken – true?' said
Brian.

'True,' they all said.

'Then we must mend it,' said Brian.
'Simple!'

21

He looked round triumphantly.

'How about a round of applause?' he said.

'How about a thump on the bonce?' said Dougal.

'Dougal!' said Florence. 'Don't be vulgar,' and she explained to Brian that mending the Roundabout had occurred to all of them; they were just thinking about the best way to do it.

'Oh, sorry,' said Brian, 'I thought perhaps the fundamentals of the problem had been overlooked.'

'Our fundamental problem is *you*,' said Dougal. 'Now be quiet and think.'

They all thought again.

'I've got it!' said Brian. 'This time I've really got it!'

'If you haven't you're going to have *something*,' said Dougal, darkly.

'No, listen,' said Brian. 'We need to mend the Roundabout – true?'

'True,' they all said.

'So why don't we ring up the Roundabout menders?' said Brian. 'Simple.'

They all thought.

'That's a great idea, man,' said Dylan, and he dropped off to sleep with relief.

'Well, I must say it does *seem* to be a good idea, small creature,' said Ermintrude.

'It's a *possibility*,' said Mr Rusty, thought-fully.

'Yes, a possibility,' said Florence.

Dougal got up and went over to Brian.

'Snail,' he said, 'you have a great talent.'

'Thank you,' said Brian, proudly.

'There are just one or two minor points I should like to raise,' said Dougal.

'Raise them,' said Brian, confidently.

'One,' said Dougal, 'we don't know any Roundabout menders to ring up.

'Two – I doubt if anyone knows any Roundabout menders to ring up.

'Three – I doubt if there *are* any Roundabout menders who could be rung up.

'Four, we haven't got a telephone book and five, WE HAVEN'T GOT A TELEPHONE ! ! ! !'

'Steady, Dougal,' murmured Florence.

'Well!' said Dougal. 'It's always the same. Roundabout menders, indeed!! Really!! Now let's all think sensibly about what to do. You too!!' he said to Brian.

But Brian had gone.

'Where's he gone?' said Dougal.

'He said he wouldn't be a minute,' said Mr Rusty.

'Well, at least we can think in peace,' said Dougal.

And they all thought again.

There was a rumble in the distance.

'Not another thunderstorm, I hope,' said Mr Rusty, nervously.

'I think it's the train, dear heart,' said Ermintrude.

But it wasn't, it was a lorry.

It got nearer and nearer.

It was a very old lorry and it made a lot of noise. It came to a halt by the Roundabout, steam sizzling out of the radiator and the engine making all sorts of suspicious noises. Painted on the side was:

'I don't believe it,' squeaked Dougal.

'What a coincidence,' said Florence.

But it wasn't a coincidence because Brian got out of the lorry.

'Friends of mine,' he said. 'Not a lot of work on at the moment – able to come at once to our assistance. May I introduce Mr Nettleship and Mr Butt.'

Two very old men got out of the lorry.

One was very tall and the other was very short, and they were both dressed in long overalls and big boots.

'Roundabout menders,' said Brian, looking at Dougal.

Dougal sighed.

'You can't win, can you?' he said to
Florence.

'Cheer up, Dougal,' said Florence.

Mr Rusty explained the problem to the
Roundabout menders and Mr Nettleship and
Mr Butt walked round looking at the damage.

'1913 model?' said Mr Nettleship.

'More like 1915, I'd say,' said Mr Butt.

'With respect, Gasgoigne,' said Mr
Nettleship, 'I think you're wrong.'

'And with respect, Ron,' said Mr Butt, 'I
think I'm right.'

'Er . . . it's a 1914 model,' said Mr Rusty.

'Ah!' said Mr Nettleship and Mr Butt. 'Ah!'

'Then it's got self-winding elastic sprockets,' said Mr Butt.

'And apple-wood connections to the rollers,' said Mr Nettleship.

'Ah!' they both said again.

Dougal and Brian giggled like anything.

'I wonder if it's got fur-lined quonkers?' said Brian.

'Or gronge-grabbers on the waffles?' said Dougal.

And they both fell about laughing like anything.

'Quiet, you two!' said Florence, sharply.

'Sorry,' they said, giggling.

Everyone sat down to watch the experts at work.

Mr Nettleship and Mr Butt walked over to their lorry and pulled out two big bags of tools.

'I think the first problem is to stabilise the equilibrium joints,' said Mr Nettleship.

'Indubitably,' said Mr Butt.

'We shall need a little assistance,' they said.

Everyone was very ready to help.

'Now to get at the equilibrium joints we need the Roundabout on its side,' said Mr Butt. 'This means attaching a rope to the top, giving a hearty pull and putting a wedge underneath.'

So they attached a rope to the top and gave a hearty pull.

The Roundabout fell over.

'Was that a bit too hearty?' said Brian.

'Get it off me!' screeched Dougal.

'Oh dear, Dougal,' said Florence, 'are you all right?'

'I'm as all right as anyone could be with a roundabout on top of him,' huffed Dougal.

Mr Nettleship and Mr Butt came round to look.

'If you could stay there for a little while,' they said to Dougal, 'it will greatly assist us. We have the machine at just the right angle. You are, if anything, better than a wedge.'

'I'm so glad,' said Dougal.

'It's nice to be useful, isn't it?' said Brian, brightly.

'Go away,' said Dougal.

The Roundabout menders got to work. All sorts of tools came out of the tool-bags and there was a lot of banging and crashing and wrenching.

'May I trouble you for the pinchers, Ron?' said Mr Butt.

'Certainly, Gasgoigne,' said Mr Nettleship, passing them.

The work went on and the Roundabout gradually took shape again. A final twist and the last bend was straightened.

'There, then,' said Mr Butt.

'Perfect,' said Mr Nettleship.

'Er . . . finished?' said Mr Rusty.

They said they were. All that was needed was to put the Roundabout the right way up and test it for stability and accuracy. Another good pull on the rope was needed.

Everyone got hold of the rope and pulled. The Roundabout straightened up with a jerk, and Dougal flipped straight up into the air and landed quivering on the top.

'Get me down!' he shrieked.

But before anyone could stop them Mr

Nettleship and Mr Butt were testing the Roundabout for stability and accuracy. They made it go very fast and then they made it go very slow and then they made it go very fast again. Finally they stopped it.

'It's all right now,' they said, 'except for one small thing.'

'What's that?' said Mr Rusty.

'That mascot on the top is too heavy in our opinion. It spoils the accuracy of the plonk-bearings. It should be replaced – perhaps by a small flag.'

'I'm not a mascot,' screamed Dougal. 'I'm here by accident!! And I feel very sick!!'

'You look lovely,' shouted Brian.

'I'm not interested in your opinion,' shouted Dougal. 'Get a ladder!!'

They got a ladder and Dougal was helped down. He sat on the ground quivering.

'Now I don't wish to complain,' he said. 'You know me, no one could be less complaining. But I have been used as a wedge. I have been used as a test for stability and equilibrium – would it be too much to ask if anyone is thinking of making a cup of tea?'

'I could do you a lettuce butty,' said Brian, brightly.

But Florence realised Dougal's needs and everyone went into Mr Rusty's place for tea. Mr Nettleship and Mr Butt had a cup each and then said they had to go.

'Got a big job on in Stockport,' they said.

Everyone waved goodbye as the lorry rattled away.

'Er . . . anyone feel like a ride on the Roundabout?' said Mr Rusty.

'I think I'll just have another cup of tea and watch,' said Dougal.

Which he did.

The Scarecrow

The next day Dougal felt the need for a little solitude and relaxation. What with the great storm and the Roundabout repairs life had been a trifle hectic.

'I need to get away on my own,' he thought. 'I need to wind down. I need peace.'

So after having breakfast he packed a little haversack with a few sustaining odds and ends like a flask of tea and a packet of Eccles cakes, and set off for a quiet walk in the country.

He hadn't gone far when he met Brian.

'Good morrow, striding chum,' said Brian.

Dougal grunted and went on.

'Going somewhere?' called Brian.

Dougal didn't answer.

'Can I come?' shouted Brian.

Dougal stopped and went slowly back to Brian. He got very close to him and looked him straight in the eye.

'No,' he said, and strode away again.

'I couldn't anyway,' shouted Brian. 'I'm busy.'

Dougal went on, muttering.

'That's all I need,' he said. 'A snail for company. I'd probably only get as far as the gate.'

He reached the top of a hill and breathed deeply. The air was very fresh and the sun was very warm. Dougal felt relaxed and contented.

'I should do this more often,' he thought, nibbling an Eccles cake. 'Commune with nature. Get back to the grass roots. Get away from it all.'

He sighed happily and strode down the hill.

'I feel somehow it's going to be a good day.'

He came to a cross-roads and wondered which way to go. Both ways looked green and inviting and good for walking along.

'Oh dear, decisions, decisions! You can't get away from them,' he sighed. 'I shall wait here and ask some passing rustic for advice.'

33

He sat down beside the road and had a cup of tea out of his flask. The sun shone and the birds sang – it was very peaceful.

Along the lane came a herd of cows. They were talking amongst themselves and browsing occasionally on the grass verges.

'Good morning, ladies,' said Dougal.

The cows looked at him and started giggling amongst themselves.

'Er . . . could you tell me a good way to go for a walk?' said Dougal.

'Have you tried putting one foot in front of another?' said one of the cows, and the whole herd fell about the road laughing like anything.

Dougal waited until they stopped.

'You have misunderstood me,' he said, icily.

'I just want to know a good place for walking.'

'Sorry, we're strangers here,' said the cows, and they went on munching and giggling.

'Typical!' said Dougal. 'Typical!'

Then he saw a man wandering along behind the cows.

'Er . . . excuse me, sir,' he said. 'I should like a little advice.'

'Oh, ar?' said the man. 'Oh, ar . . . err . . . ar?'

'Er . . . yes,' said Dougal, 'I'm out for a walk and I wondered if you could tell me a good way to go for . . . er . . . the best scenery and that sort of thing.'

'Ah . . .' said the man. 'Oh, ar . . . err . . . ar! Yus . . . ar! Depends . . .'

'Depends on what?' said Dougal.

'Whether you'm wantin' the deloights of the woodylands or the grand vastiness of the open fields,' said the man.

'Well, let's say the grand vastiness of the open fields,' said Dougal.

'Ah, yus!' said the man. 'Ar . . . ar! Well, that's a bitty difficult, loike.'

'Well, if you could just show me the bitty . . . I mean . . . er . . . the best way to get there,' said Dougal.

'Walkin', are you?' said the man.

'No,' said Dougal, sarcastically, 'I've got this three-ton lorry and trailer with me.'

The man thought about this.

'You'm 'avin' me on,' he said at last.

Dougal sighed.

'Goodbye,' he said.

'Arf a mo,' said the man. 'Arf a little mo. There is one bitty of advice I can give you.'

'Yes?' said Dougal.

'You want to go to Lower Bogweed – great place for walkin',' said the man.

'How do I get there?' said Dougal.

'Ah!' said the man. 'That's the thing.'

'I thought it might be,' said Dougal.

'No, that's the trouble,' said the man. 'Ow to get there, loike.'

'Bitty difficult?' asked Dougal.

'Just a bitty,' said the man. 'In fact . . .'

He scratched his head.

'In *fact*,' he said, 'if I was you, I wouldn't start from here at all.'

'Thank you,' said Dougal, heavily.

'You'm more'n welcome,' said the man.

And he went on his way after the cows.

Dougal went the other way. It seemed the only thing to do under the circumstances and he didn't want to catch up with the herd of cows.

He came to a gate. It led into a field and in the middle of the field was a figure.

'I'll have one more try,' said Dougal, 'and then I'll give up.'

He went towards the figure. It was standing quite still with its arms outstretched. It was a scarecrow.

'Er . . . excuse me,' said Dougal, 'I'm a stranger in these parts and . . .'

'Sh!!' said the scarecrow suddenly. 'Sh!! Do you hear anything?'

Dougal listened.

'No,' he said.

'Oh, I thought I heard a crow,' said the scarecrow. 'Never mind.'

Dougal gazed round the empty field. Not a bird of any sort was in sight.

'You seem to be doing a remarkably good job,' he said. 'You must be very proud.'

The scarecrow looked at him and then suddenly burst into tears.

'Oh, it's awful!' he wailed. 'Awful. I must be the loneliest creature in the world. Everyone hates me. No one comes to see me. Even the birds avoid me. Boo! Hoo!'

'Now steady on,' said Dougal, 'surely that's your job, isn't it – to frighten away the birds?'

'I know, that's what makes it so awful,' said the scarecrow. 'If they only knew I wouldn't do them any harm they wouldn't be frightened. Then I'd have a few visitors – a crow or two perched on my arms and perhaps a pigeon on my hat.'

He cried some more.

'It's not fair!' he said. 'It's discrimination.'

'Look,' said Dougal, 'I don't wish to appear unsympathetic, but if you were visited by the crows you wouldn't be any good as a scarecrow, would you? You don't want to be a failure, do you?'

'I'd rather be a failure than lonely!' moaned the scarecrow.

'Just my luck,' thought Dougal, 'to encounter a crazy mixed-up scarecrow.'

The scarecrow cried louder.

'I want to be liked!' he wailed. 'I want to be visited and appreciated!!'

'All right! All right!' said Dougal. 'Stop crying and I'll see what I can do.'

The scarecrow gave a sniff and looked a little brighter.

'Will you?' he said. 'Promise?'

Dougal opened his haversack.

'It seems to me that your problem is one of supply and demand,' he said. 'There doesn't seem to be much in this field to attract the birds, so I'm going to scatter a few goodies.'

He crumbled up the last of the Eccles cakes and scattered them on the ground around the scarecrow.

'Put a few pieces on my hat,' said the scarecrow. 'On the hat! On the hat!'

Dougal put a few pieces on the hat.

'And along the arms!' said the scarecrow, delightedly. Dougal did so.

'Oh, I was lucky to meet you,' said the scarecrow. 'You're a real friend.'

'Oh, don't mention it,' said Dougal. 'I just hope I don't faint with hunger on the way home, that's all.'

He bent down to put the empty paper-bag in his haversack, and was suddenly knocked over and rolled along the ground.

'What! What! What!' he shrieked. 'What!?'

The sky was full of crows and starlings and pigeons and sparrows, all cawing and cooing and cheeping excitedly.

Dougal jumped up. Seven crows were inside his haversack pecking away at the paper-bag, and three pigeons were trying to get the top off his vacuum flask.

'Leave my tea alone, you vandals!' he shrieked.

More and more birds arrived. The scarecrow was beside himself with delight. There were crows perched all along his arms, his hat had seven starlings on it and his pockets were full of sparrows.

A rook jumped on to Dougal's head.

'Got any more cake?' it asked.

'No,' said Dougal, 'not a crumb.'

'I don't think he's telling the truth,' said a robin.

'I am! I am!' said Dougal, backing away. He picked up his haversack and ran, the birds cawing and cooing and tweeting and laughing.

'Thank you very much!' shouted the scarecrow.

Dougal got out of the gate and went very fast down the lane.

'The things I do!' he muttered.

He met the herd of cows coming back. As soon as they saw him they started giggling again.

'Had a good walk?' they mooed. 'Putting your best foot forward?'

They all laughed a great deal again and went on.

The man was following behind.

'Ar . . . !' he said. 'Ar!'

'Oh, ar!' said Dougal, without stopping.

He got back to the garden and met Brian.

'Had a good time?' asked Brian.

'Wonderful,' said Dougal. 'Very refreshing.'

'We've had a bit of excitement here,' said Brian. 'Great flocks of birds. They've eaten all Mr MacHenry's currants. And I think they got into your biscuit tin too.'

'What!?' screeched Dougal. 'My biccies?'

He rushed to his house. There was his biscuit tin empty except for one black feather.

'We shall have to get a scarecrow,' said Brian. 'Want to come back to my place for tea?'

'I wouldn't mind,' said Dougal, heavily.

'I think I've got an Eccles cake left,' said Brian. 'We could have it with lettuce.'

So they did.

The Run

Dougal was having breakfast. With a sigh of contentment he finished his last cup of tea and was just about to pop his final piece of toast and marmalade in his mouth when the door burst open.

It was Brian.

'STOP!' he cried.

Dougal gave a great jump, the piece of toast and marmalade missed his mouth and stuck stickily on the end of his nose.

'What?!' he screeched. 'What?! What?!'

Brian came into the room.

'STOP!' he said, sternly.

Dougal controlled himself.

'Stop *what*?' he asked, icily.

'All this eating,' said Brian. 'All this eating and drinking and . . . er . . . eating.'

He sat down.

'You've got a piece of toast on your nose,' he said. 'Did you know?'

Dougal said nothing, but removed the piece of toast and put it on his plate.

'You've also got some marmalade on your
nose,' said Brian. 'Did you know that?'

Dougal stretched out his tongue and licked
the marmalade off.

'I say, that was pretty nasty to watch,' said
Brian.

'Then avert your gaze,' said Dougal, licking
some more.

He picked up the piece of toast.

'STOP!!' said Brian, loudly.

This time the piece of toast hurtled across the
room and landed in the coal bucket.

'Sorry,' said Brian, 'did I make you jump?'

'Oh no,' said Dougal, 'I'm used to having
snails leaping about at breakfast time and

shouting "STOP" every time I try to eat a piece of toast – I'm used to it, it doesn't bother me a bit. Great oaf!'

He started to pour another cup of tea.

'Stop that too!' said Brian, sternly.

Dougal put down the teapot with a clatter.

'Snail,' he said quietly, 'in a moment I am going to get up out of this chair and I am going to take hold of you quite firmly and cover you with marmalade.'

'I say, that's a bit worrying,' said Brian. 'Why should you want to do that?'

'Because I'm like that,' said Dougal.

'Sometimes I like to spread marmalade over everything. So unless you want to end up very sticky, you'd better tell me what this is all about.'

'All what?' said Brian.

'All this screeching "STOP" whenever I want a piece of toast or a cup of tea,' said Dougal.

'Ah,' said Brian, 'ah, yes. It's very important and I thought you'd never ask me.'

'I'm asking,' said Dougal.

'Diet,' said Brian.

There was a pause. It was very quiet – just the clock ticking and the kettle sizzling gently.

'I hope you're not implying that *I* need to diet,' said Dougal, quietly.

'Well . . .' said Brian.

'Or that I'm *fat*,' said Dougal.

'Well . . .' said Brian.

'Or that I'm not everything a healthy dog should be?' said Dougal.

'Well . . .' said Brian.

'Because if you *are*,' said Dougal, 'I don't fancy your chances of getting out of that door.'

'No, listen, old chum,' said Brian, nervously, 'I'm not implying anything. It's just that diet is important, and of course you know *me* – far be it from me to repeat what other people say – you know *me*, nothing would be further from my mind, but . . .'

'*People* are saying that I'm fat?' said Dougal, fiercely.

'You're being a bit fierce,' said Brian.

'I'm always fierce when people call me fat,' said Dougal.

'Well, not *fat*,' said Brian, '. . . er . . . just . . . er . . . well covered.'

'Who's been saying it?' demanded Dougal.

'Oh, I've just heard the odd remark, you *know*,' said Brian, 'but the important thing is diet. No more bread, no more marmalade, no more biscuits, no more cream buns, no more sugar . . .'

Dougal began to go very pale . . .

'No more tea,' continued Brian, 'no more chips, no more sweeties, no more orange squish.'

Dougal seemed to get smaller and smaller . . .

'And above all,' said Brian, 'no more sitting around watching telly. Exercise is the keynote.'

'Exercise?' said Dougal, faintly.

'*Ex-er-cise*!' said Brian. 'A good diet and lots of exercise make a dog healthy, wealthy and wise.'

'What about snails?' said Dougal.

'We are slim and healthy by nature,' said Brian. 'So, if you're ready?'

'Ready for what?' said Dougal.

'Your two-mile run,' said Brian.

'TWO-MILE RUN!' said Dougal.

'Two miles at least,' said Brian, 'and then back home for a glass of water, two lettuce leaves and as a special treat – an apple.'

'If you think that I'm getting up and going for a two-mile run you must be dotty,' said Dougal.

'Ah, well,' said Brian, 'it's up to you, of course. Everyone will be very disappointed.'

'That's their problem,' said Dougal.

'But everyone else is going for a two-mile run,' said Brian. 'I'll just go and tell them that you think you're all right as you are, shall I?'

Dougal thought about this.

'I'll be there,' he sighed.

'I'll go and tell them,' said Brian. 'They'll be *very* pleased.'

He went out and closed the door.

Dougal waited a moment, then opened his biscuit tin.

'Better have a little something to sustain me,' he muttered.

'No secret nibbling said Brian sternly, looking in the window

Dougal dropped the tin with a crash.

'I wasn't! Er . . . I wouldn't . . . er . . . Oh, go away!' he said.

'I'll wait for you,' said Brian, significantly. 'Get your shorts on.'

'What do I need shorts for?' demanded Dougal.

'You can't run without shorts,' said Brian. 'It's not done.'

'Well, I *walk* without shorts,' said Dougal.

'That's different,' said Brian. 'Everyone will be wearing shorts – you don't want to be laughed at, do you?'

Dougal sighed and rummaged in his drawer. He found a pair of tartan shorts and pulled them on.

'Come on then, lightning,' he said, and they went to join the others.

Everyone was assembled at Mr Rusty's house. Mr Rusty and Mr MacHenry were talking about how it was much too late in life for them to think about dieting and going for runs, but what a good thing it was all the young ones were so enthusiastic.

No one *seemed* very enthusiastic.

Dylan was leaning against a tree wearing shorts and a vest with 'YALE' written on the front and 'LEEDS' on the back.

Florence was wearing shorts and a hanky round her head to keep her hair out of the way.

Ermintrude's shorts were very voluminous and marked 'SMITHFIELD 1938'.

Everyone greeted Dougal and Brian.

'All here now?' asked Mr Rusty.

Everyone said they were.

'Well, as you know,' said Mr Rusty, 'this is the first run of many we are going to have.'

'No, I jolly well *didn't* know,' said Dougal.

'Hush, Dougal,' said Florence, jumping up and down.

'I shall blow this whistle,' continued Mr Rusty, 'and you will all start.'

Everyone lined up. Brian was next to Dougal.

'Fun, isn't it?' he said.

'You're not going, are you?' said Dougal.

'Why not?' said Brian.

'But snails can't run,' said Dougal. 'It's a well known fact.'

'Have you ever seen a snail running?' said Brian.

'No,' said Dougal.

'Well then,' said Brian, and when Mr Rusty blew his whistle he set off at a great pace.

Dylan started fast as well and Florence kept up with him. Ermintrude went off at a sedate gallop and everyone disappeared over the brow of a hill.

All except Dougal.

'Aren't you going?' said Mr MacHenry, anxiously.

'In my own good time,' said Dougal and he wandered slowly after the others, thinking.

He got to the top of the hill. All the others were mere specks in the distance.

'They'll do themselves a mischief,' he thought, giggling.

But then he thought the others would be expecting him to catch up.

'Um . . .' he muttered, 'this calls for guile. Now, let me think . . .'

Meanwhile the others were carrying on. As

they crossed a ploughed field they got muddier and muddier.

Brian, being closest to the ground, was muddiest of all.

'Fun, isn't it?' he said, bravely.

They plodded on, squelching a lot and wondering what had happened to Dougal.

Suddenly Ermintrude stopped.

'Now wait a little moment,' she said.

They all stopped.

'Now, as you know, I'm not one for beating about the bush,' said Ermintrude, 'and I don't mind saying I'm not enjoying this one little bit. Exercise is one thing but squelching in the mud is quite another. I think we should go back to the garden and have a bath and some tea.'

Everyone was very glad someone had been brave enough to say what they'd all been thinking.

'Yes, let's go back,' they said.

'What about Dougal?' said Florence.

They looked around. There was no sign of Dougal.

'The dear thing will catch up,' said Ermintrude, 'so all get on and I'll give you a ride home.'

'That's very kind, mam,' murmured Dylan.

'Well, I'm biggest,' said Ermintrude.

So Dylan and Florence and Brian climbed on to Ermintrude's back and they set off at a trot, covered in mud and very glad to be going back.

Meanwhile Dougal had thought and had come up with a splendid idea. He had crept back to the starting line and had borrowed Mr MacHenry's motor-bike without Mr MacHenry seeing him. He was now speeding along chortling.

'Two miles is two miles,' he giggled. 'No one actually said it had to be done on *foot*.'

Ermintrude and the others were coming back.

Dougal was racing towards them.

They were both on the same road.

They met face to face. Dougal stopped and looked. Ermintrude, with the others riding on her back and all covered in mud, was quite unrecognisable. She looked like a mythical beast with horns and three humps.

'Er . . . hallo,' said Dougal, nervously, not
knowing who it was.

Ermintrude nodded, looking at Dougal's
motor-bike.

'Er . . . you haven't by any chance seen
anyone *running*, have you?' said Dougal.

Ermintrude shook her head. So did Florence
and Dylan and Brian. It was a very strange sight.

Dougal got back on his machine.

'Thank you,' he said, and went.

'Well!' said Brian. 'A motor-bike! The cheat ! !'

'What a *monster*!' said Ermintrude.

'Like . . . deceptive . . .' said Dylan.

'I shall speak to him severely,' said Florence.

And they went back to the garden.

Dougal meanwhile was having a little trouble with Mr MacHenry's motor-bike. It was puttering and spluttering like anything, and finally it stopped.

Dougal looked in the petrol tank. Plenty of petrol. He looked at the engine. Nothing seemed to be loose.

'Oh, curses!' said Dougal, and he gave the bike a little kick. It roared into life and shot away down the hill like a mad thing, leaving Dougal behind.

'Stop!' shouted Dougal
'Stop!'

But it didn't stop. Dougal started running after it.

'Stop that machine!' he shouted, but there was no one about to hear him.

The motor-bike went on and on. Across a ploughed field and through streams and bushes – Dougal racing along behind.

Finally the machine slowed down, hit a tree, fell over and stopped. Dougal panted up and sat down beside it.

'Oooh, I hate machinery!' he groaned, trying to get his breath back. He stood the motor-bike up and tried to start it. It wouldn't. He looked in the petrol tank. Empty.

'I don't believe it,' he whispered. 'I just don't believe it. Miles from anywhere with an empty tank. Really, the things that happen to me.'

He started to walk, pushing the motor-bike and groaning heavily.

Meanwhile, back in the garden, everyone had cleaned up and Mr Rusty was providing tea and cakes.

They all sat down to wait for Dougal.

'I expect he'll come running in soon,' said Brian, 'saying how fit he feels.'

'I wonder what he'll do with my motor-bike,' said Mr MacHenry.

'Hide it, I expect,' they said.

They waited. In the distance a little speck appeared. It got nearer and nearer. It was Dougal, pushing the motor-bike and completely covered in mud.

He arrived and sat down.

'That's it,' he said. 'That's absolutely it. No more running for me.',

'But you didn't run,' they said, accusingly, 'you used Mr MacHenry's motor-bike.'

'That motor-bike ran away from me,' said Dougal, 'and I chased it for about ten miles before it ran out of petrol. AND I've pushed it all the way home, and anyway how did you know?' He looked around suspiciously.

'Er . . . we saw you,' said Brian, 'from a point of vantage.'

Florence looked thoughtful, remembering the ride home.

'I think it would be best,' she said slowly, 'if we forgot all about who ran where.'

'I've forgotten,' said Dougal. 'I'd rather be fat and happy. Any cake?'

There was.

The Rugger Match

Dougal was having his breakfast and reading the paper. Opposite him Brian, who had called early for a cup of tea, was trying to read the back page.

'You're a very jerky reader,' he said. 'Can't you keep still a minute?'

Dougal looked over the top of the paper.

'Snail,' he said, 'don't push your luck. You are here having a slice of my toast and a cup of my tea. If you want to read a paper go and buy one.'

Brian sighed.

'You're very hard sometimes,' he said.

Then he caught sight of a headline on the back page. He got up on the table to look at it more closely.

'Cor,' he said. 'How interesting!'

Dougal lowered the paper and found himself face to face with Brian very close.

'Eek!' he screeched. 'What's *that*!?'

'It's only me,' said Brian.

'Oh, I do wish you wouldn't *creep up*,' said Dougal. 'My nerves won't stand it this early in the morning.'

'But have you seen this?' Brian said excitedly, and he knocked the paper round and pointed with his head.

Dougal read.

'SCOTS ROUTED' 'FRENCH VICTORY BY 58 POINTS' 'WHAT'S WRONG WITH SCOTLAND?' 'ARCHIE MACFEE REPORTS'

Dougal went quite pale.

'I don't believe it,' he whispered. 'I just don't believe it.'

'I wouldn't believe it if I knew what it meant,' said Brian, happily.

'It must be a mistake,' said Dougal in a strangled voice.

'Is it war?' said Brian.

'No, you oaf, it's Rugger,' said Dougal. 'Rugby Football. We've been beaten by the French.'

'Is that bad?' said Brian.

'OF COURSE IT'S BAD!' said Dougal. 'IT'S DISASTROUS! 58 POINTS! IT'S HUMILIATING! GRRR!!!'

He gulped another cup of tea, choked, ran around the room tearing the paper into little shreds and finally sat down, panting.

'I say, steady on,' said Brian. 'You've gone quite red.'

'I'm not surprised,' said Dougal. 'Pour me another cup of tea.'

Brian peered.

'There's none left,' he said.

'Oh, it's all too much,' groaned Dougal. 'Beaten by the French and now no tea left.'

'You could make some more,' said Brian, reasonably.

'I don't feel up to it,' said Dougal. 'I'm drained. I'm a husk.'

He slumped in his chair.

'They're good at this Rugger thing then, the French?' said Brian, brightly.

'Yes,' sighed Dougal.

'And the Scotch are rotten at it?' said Brian.

'Scots,' corrected Dougal, 'not Scotch. Always says Scots – or Scottish.'

'And the Scots or Scottish are rotten at it then?' said Brian.

'No, they are not!' said Dougal. 'Obviously something went very wrong.'

'*You* weren't playing,' said Brian.

'Well,' said Dougal, 'I wouldn't like to say *that*, but ...' He gave a little cough, '... it might have made a difference.'

'Why weren't you playing?' asked Brian.

Dougal slumped further.

'I wasn't asked,' he groaned.

Brian got up and moved about the room, thinking.

'I'm thinking,' he said, 'and I believe I have one of my jolly little ideas.'

'I can't wait to hear it,' said Dougal.

'Why don't *we* give it a go?' said Brian.

'Give what a go?' said Dougal.

'This Rugger lark,' said Brian. 'We could make up a team and defeat the perfidious Frenchymen. We could kick 'em and whack 'em and totally defeat 'em by hundreds and hundreds and hundreds of points . . . and that.'

Dougal looked at him pityingly.

'Have you ever played Rugger?' he asked.

'Well, *no*,' said Brian, 'not actually played – but I'm nippy with a ball.'

'You'd be more nippy *as* a ball,' said Dougal.

'No, don't be rotten,' said Brian. 'I bet we could do it.'

Dougal thought.

'You know, mollusc,' he said, 'you may have something. We could make up a five-a-side team and issue a challenge. Do you think there are five of us who could play?'

Brian got very excited.

'You get in touch with those Frenchmen,' he said, 'and I'll go and rally up a team.'

He rushed to the door.

'Er . . . you'll be captain, I suppose?' he said.

'Naturally,' said Dougal. 'Who else? Go! Go! Go!'

So Brian went, leaving Dougal to arrange the match.

Florence and the others were a little dubious about the whole thing when Brian explained the situation.

'It's for the honour of Scotland,' said Brian.

'But I'm English,' said Florence.

'And I'm . . . like . . . American,' said Dylan.

'And I'm not sure what I am,' said Ermintrude, 'but I've never felt particularly Scottish.'

'Oh, now look, that's not the point,' said Brian. 'Are we going to let our lovely friend *down*. He is relying on us. We are his *chums*.'

So they all said in that case they would be perfectly willing to help out and when was the match to be?

'It's being arranged,' said Brian.

'What do we wear, dear thing?' said Ermintrude.

'Er . . . I don't know,' said Brian.

'Then we'd all better have a rummage around and meet back here,' said Ermintrude.

'There's just one thing more,' said Florence, thoughtfully.

'Yes?' said Brian.

'How do we play this game?' said Florence.

'I haven't the remotest idea,' said Brian, 'but it's a *ball* game so it can't be very complicated. Anyway our friend will explain. All go and get ready and meet back here.'

Meanwhile Dougal had contacted the French Rugby Football Team and issued the challenge.

He arrived in the garden to find Brian assembling the team.

'ALL LINE UP FOR THE CAPTAIN'S INSPECTION!' shouted Brian.

They all lined up.

Dougal looked at them.

Ermintrude, uncertain as to the rules of the game but certain that Frenchmen were to be present, had put on a large flowered hat and high-heeled shoes.

Dylan, remembering his American connections, was well padded on the shoulders and knees and was wearing a large helmet.

Florence had just put a new bow in her hair, and Brian had painted a large number 3 on his shell.

Dougal walked slowly down the line, and then took a deep breath.

'Never in the history of Rugby Football,' he

said, 'was so much incompetence displayed by so few for the honour of so many.'

'SCOTLAND FOR EVER!' shouted Brian. 'Hip! Hip! HOORAY!!'

'Oh, shut up!' said Dougal.

'Ooooh!!' said Brian.

'That wasn't very nice, Dougal,' said Florence.

Dougal sat down and looked at them again.

'In a moment,' he said, 'a team of five Frenchmen will arrive expecting to play a game of Rugger and they're going to find you lot. I'm not sure I can let it happen – they may injure themselves laughing.'

'Now that's not very nice, either, Dougal,' said Florence. 'We are only doing this for you.'

'And Scotland,' said Brian.

'And anyway I think it's too late now to have second thoughts, dear dog,' said Ermintrude.

She was right. A small motor-coach was approaching, the French flag flying from its bonnet and faint sounds of the Marseillaise coming from inside.

Dougal paled, gulped and went forward to meet their opponents. The coach stopped, the door opened and out stepped five of the biggest men Dougal had ever seen in his life. They were huge and they all looked very fierce.

68

'Oh my!' murmured Ermintrude.

'Gracious!' said Florence.

'Golly!' said Brian.

Dougal bowed.

'Er . . . welcome,' he said.

The biggest Frenchman stepped forward.

'Merci,' he said, looking at Dougal's team lined up.

'What's he looking at us like that for?' hissed Brian, nervously.

'I can't imagine,' said Ermintrude.

The Frenchman came slowly forward, kissed Florence on both cheeks, patted Brian on the shell, saluted Ermintrude and shook Dylan by the hand. Then he went back to his team and they all went into a huddle.

Dougal came across to *his* team.

'What are they doing?' whispered Brian.

'They didn't say,' hissed Dougal.

They all watched. The Frenchmen finished huddling and started throwing a ball between themselves, laughing.

'I don't like the sound of that laugh, for a start,' said Brian.

'Dougal, are you sure this is *wise*?' said Florence.

Dougal gulped again.

'It's too late now,' he said.

'Er . . . ready?' he called.

'Oui,' said the Frenchmen.

'They don't look very wee to me,' said Brian.

'I think that's French for "yes",' said Florence.

'Oh,' said Brian. 'What a funny lot.'

'We are in readiness,' said the French captain, and he threw the ball over. It caught Dougal in the midriff, and lifted him three feet in the air.

'Ooof!' he said.

The Frenchmen came across.

'We start,' they said. 'Where is the field of battle?'

'This way,' said Dougal, grimly struggling to get his breath back, and they all went into a small field. The Frenchmen started to run up and down very fast, passing the ball to each other and shouting a lot.

'Have they started?' said Brian.

'I think they're just practising,' said Florence.

Mr MacHenry came along.

'What's all this?' he said, and they explained.

'Who's the referee?' asked Mr MacHenry.

'You are,' they said.

'Then it was lucky I came along, wasn't it?' said Mr MacHenry, and he blew a piercing blast on a whistle and rode into the middle of the field on his motor-bike.

'Kick off!' he called.

Everyone lined up and one of the Frenchmen took a great kick at the ball. It went up into the air and disappeared. All the French team rushed down the field, leaving Dougal and the others standing quite still.

'After them!' shouted Dougal, setting off at a run.

But he was too late. The ball came down, one

71

of the French team caught it and threw himself on the ground with a great shout.

'Try,' said Mr MacHenry.

'We are trying,' said Brian.

'No, I mean that's a "try" to them – four points,' said Mr MacHenry.

'When you score a "try" you get four points. We haven't got any goal-posts so we won't have any conversions.'

'What's a conversion?' said Brian.

'Oh, stop bothering,' said Dougal.

'I'd like to have been converted,' said Brian.

'That'll be the day,' said Dougal.

They all trudged back to the centre of the field. Mr MacHenry blew his whistle and the same thing happened all over again.

'Eight points to nil,' said Mr MacHenry. 'Restart.'

It happened again and again and again, the Frenchmen always rushing away with the ball, leaving Dougal's team standing quite still.

'Twenty points to nil,' said Mr MacHenry after th fifth time. 'Restart.'

'We're not doing very well, are we?' said Brian, brightly.

'NO, WE ARE NOT!' said Dougal. 'IT'S HOPELESS!!'

'Restart!' said Mr MacHenry, blowing his whistle.

The ball was kicked again. This time it went straight up in the air and started to come down towards Brian.

'Catch it!' screeched Dougal.

But Brian, seeing the ball hurtling down towards him, disappeared into his shell. The ball landed beside him. The French captain rushed up, looked at the ball, looked at Brian rolled up, picked up Brian and started to rush away. Dougal gave a shout of triumph, picked up the ball and rushed the other way followed by Ermintrude, Florence and Dylan. Dougal threw himself down with the ball.

'Try!' shouted Mr MacHenry, blowing his whistle.

'Well done, Dougal!' said Florence.

'I think we may have the answer here,' said Dougal, thoughtfully.

'Restart!' said Mr MacHenry.

The Frenchmen trooped back to the middle carrying Brian. They put him on the ground and were just about to give him a kick when he looked out of his shell.

'Don't you dare!' he said.

The French team looked absolutely stunned, and they all rushed around looking for the ball.

'Restart!' said Mr MacHenry, whistling.

Dougal hissed at Brian.

'Get back in!' he said.

'And get kicked?' said Brian. 'Not likely.'

'WILL YOU GET BACK IN!' said Dougal.
'Remember SCOTLAND!!'

Brian sighed and dived back into his shell.
Dougal gave him a little push. One of the
French players grabbed at Brian, started
running and bumped into Ermintrude.

'Steady, dear thing,' she murmured.

The whistle blew.

'Scrum down!' said Mr MacHenry.

'Do what, dear?' said Ermintrude.

'Scrum,' said Mr MacHenry. 'Heads
together and push!'

The Frenchmen looked at Ermintrude.
Ermintrude looked at the Frenchmen. They put
their heads together and pushed. Dougal
tossed Brian into the scrum and then raced up
the field with the ball.

'Try!' said Mr MacHenry. 'Restart!'

'How are we doing, man?' said Dylan.

'Where have you been?' demanded Dougal.

'Well, you seemed to be . . . like . . . enjoying yourselves,' said Dylan. 'I didn't like to interfere.'

'Good of you to take an interest,' said Dougal. 'Now take this ball and when I say "Run" – you run.'

'Crazy, man,' said Dylan.

The French team by this time were getting a bit bewildered. Every time they ran with the ball it turned out to be Brian, and every time Dougal's team scored a try.

'Twenty points all,' shouted Mr MacHenry. 'Restart!!'

Everyone assembled in the centre once more. Dougal put the ball on the ground beside Brian. The ball looked very like Brian.

Mr MacHenry blew his whistle. The French captain picked up the ball and raced off. Dougal chortled with glee, picked up Brian and raced off the other way.

'Where are we going?' shouted Brian.

Dougal screeched to a halt.

'What?! What?! What?!' he shouted. 'What are you doing here?!!'

'Don't ask me, I'm obviously just a plaything,' said Brian, huffily.

'AFTER THEM THEN!' shouted Dougal.
'TACKLE! TACKLE!'

The Frenchman with the ball rushed down the field. Ermintrude ambled towards him and lowered her head. The Frenchman crashed into her and the ball flew towards Florence.

'CATCH IT!' shouted Dougal.

Florence put out both hands – the ball bounced on her head, up in the air and on to Dougal's back.

'RUN, DOUGAL!' she shouted.

Dougal ran.
All five Frenchmen ran after him.
Dougal ran harder.
The Frenchmen ran
harder.

Dougal got near the end of the field
and disappeared under a pile of Frenchmen as
they all leapt upon him.

Everyone crowded round. Mr MacHenry
blew his whistle and the French team got up
one by one.

There was Dougal flat on the ground,
holding the ball and moaning.

'TRY!!' said Mr MacHenry. 'OUR TEAM WINS!!'

'Are you all right, Dougal?' said Florence.

Dougal heaved himself up.

'I shall let you know after tea,' he said.

The Frenchmen thanked them for the game, got into their coach and drove away.

'I don't think they'll forget that in a hurry,' said Brian.

'Neither will I,' said Dougal. 'Is tea ready?' And it was.

The Magic Book

Everyone had been invited to Zebedee's house to watch him do some magic tricks. He entertained them for a long time. He made balloons appear and disappear. He put big boxes into small boxes. He cut paper into pieces and made it whole again. Finally, he produced a pigeon out of a bowler hat and an egg out of Dougal's ear. It was all highly enjoyable.

'Would anyone else like to have a go?' he asked.

Brian said he would be very interested to have a go. Dougal sniggered.

'That snail couldn't produce water out of a tap,' he whispered.

'Hush, Dougal,' said Florence.

Brian stood on a stool beside Zebedee.

'For my first trick,' he said in a high-pitched voice, 'I shall produce a rabbit out of this very small paper-bag which once contained treacle toffee. The rabbit is called Fred and he's very nervous, so I shall have to ask for complete silence.'

There was a squeak of laughter from Dougal.

'*Com*plete silence,' said Brian, fiercely.

'Sorry, Houdini,' said Dougal, giggling.

'Now hush, Dougal,' said Florence.

The others told Dougal to hush as well because they all wanted Brian to go on with his trick.

'I shall go on with my trick,' said Brian, 'and produce this rabbit called Fred out of this small paper-bag.'

'What's the paper-bag called?' shouted Dougal, laughing like anything.

Everyone shushed Dougal again and Zebedee said if he promised to be quiet he could have a go later.

'Sorry all,' said Dougal. 'On, mollusc.'

Brian coughed.

'Er . . . thank you. Rabbit out of paper-bag trick coming up.'

He picked up the paper-bag, gave it a little tap with a wand and said:

'Fred – appear!'

Nothing happened. Brian peered into the bag.

'Try again, dear thing,' said Ermintrude.

Brian tried again. He tapped the paper-bag and said, louder:

'Fred – appear!!'

Again nothing happened.

'Go inside and get him!' hooted Dougal.

'Fred – appear!!!' shouted Brian, desperately.

No one noticed Zebedee's moustache give a little twitch, and suddenly the very small paper-bag burst open and a large white rabbit appeared.

'Gracious!' said Mr Rusty.

'Goodness!' said Florence.

'I don't believe it,' shouted Dougal. 'I do not believe it! IT WAS UP YOUR SLEEVE!'

'I HAVEN'T GOT ANY SLEEVES!' shouted Brian.

'THEN IT WAS IN YOUR HAT!' shouted Dougal.

'I'VE STILL GOT MY HAT ON!' screeched Brian.

'Please! Please!' said Florence. 'Don't shout!'

And everyone applauded Brian's marvellous trick while Dougal grumbled away to himself.

The white rabbit called Fred came to the edge of the table and peered.

'Dylan, baby!' he called.

Dylan woke up with a start.

'Er . . . what!? . . . like . . . what?' he said.

'It's me – Fred!' said Fred. 'How have you been?'

'Well, friend Fred!' said Dylan. 'It's been a long time. Still doing the paper-bag act?'

'Still doing it,' said Fred, happily. 'Still playing guitar?'

'Still playing, man,' said Dylan. 'How's Elsie?'

'Great, Dyl baby, great,' said Fred.

'WHO'S ELSIE!?' shrieked Dougal.

Dylan and Fred wandered off talking together while everyone else discussed how the trick could possibly have been done. Brian sat down next to Dougal.

'Good trick, eh?' he said.

Dougal glowered.

'I refuse to speak to you,' he said.

'Why, old matey?' said Brian.

'Because for one thing,' said Dougal, 'I thought that trick was very showy and vulgar, and for another thing – what happened to all that treacle toffee?'

'I ate it,' said Brian, happily.

'Typical!' said Dougal. 'I share my last cup of tea with you, but I don't get a sniff of any treacle toffee when it's going.'

'But it was a good rabbit trick though, wasn't it?' said Brian.

'Oh, be quiet,' said Dougal.

Zebedee tapped with his wand.

'Anyone else like to have a go?' he asked.

Florence said she would be interested to try and everyone applauded.

'I shall attempt a very little trick,' said Florence, modestly. 'I shall try to make someone disappear. For this I shall need a volunteer from the audience.'

There was no great rush to volunteer.

'May I have a volunteer, please?' said
Florence.

'This snail's volunteering,' shouted Dougal,
pushing Brian.

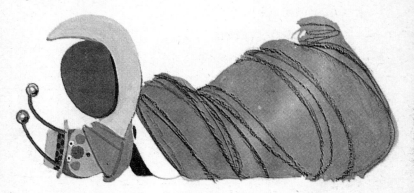

'No, I'm not,' said Brian. 'I've done my bit.
You volunteer.'

'Not likely,' said Dougal. 'I was told never to
trust ladies with wands.'

'Oh, it's quite safe,' said Florence.

'Well, in that case,' said Ermintrude bravely,
'*I* shall volunteer.'

Everyone burst out laughing, but Ermintrude
stepped on to the stage and looked round.

'I'm just as capable of disappearing as
anyone else,' she said severely. 'There's no call
for ribaldry.'

She turned to Florence.

'Ready, dear?' she said.

Florence looked a little apprehensively at Zebedee, but Zebedee gave her a little wink of reassurance.

'Go ahead,' he said.

Florence waved the wand nervously. Nothing happened.

'Shouldn't you put me in a box or something, dear heart?' said Ermintrude.

'I haven't got a box,' said Florence.

'Use the table-cloth!' shouted Dougal, helpless with laughter.

'Or a match-box,' shouted Brian, wheezing and giggling.

Ermintrude told Dougal and Brian to be quiet.

'*Try* the table-cloth,' she said to Florence.

Florence threw the table-cloth over Ermintrude. It didn't cover her completely – her legs and tail still showed.

'She's still there!' shrieked Brian and Dougal, laughing.

'I haven't started yet,' said Florence.

'Oh, sorry,' they said, tittering.

Florence walked slowly round Ermintrude tapping her with the wand.

'Ermintrude, disappear!' she said.

Zebedee's moustache gave another little twitch, and suddenly Ermintrude's legs disappeared leaving the table-cloth with Ermintrude inside it apparently suspended in mid-air.

'Have I gone, dear?' said Ermintrude.

'Not exactly,' said Florence.

Dougal and Brian were finding it difficult to contain themselves.

'No visible means of support!' they shrieked, holding on to each other and crying with laughter.

Florence tapped again. This time Ermintrude's legs reappeared and her body disappeared, leaving the table-cloth just like a table with four legs and a tail.

Everyone roared with laughter.

'What time's tea?' hooted Dougal.

'I ain't got no body!' screamed Brian, and they both laughed so much they ended up in a heap on the floor.

'What's happening now, dear?' said Ermintrude.

'I'm not sure,' said Florence, desperately.

She gave a further tap just as Zebedee's moustache gave another twitch, and this time the table-cloth floated to the ground and Ermintrude, with a faint 'moo', was gone completely.

Everyone gathered round. Mr Rusty lifted up the table-cloth. Ermintrude certainly wasn't there.

'What a marvellous trick,' said Mr Rusty.

'Marvellous,' said Mr MacHenry.

Dougal looked at Brian and Brian looked at Dougal.

'All right then,' they said. 'BRING HER BACK!!'

Florence laughed and so did Zebedee, and then Dougal realised *Zebedee* had done the trick and Zebedee had done the rabbit trick too.

'It was *you*,' he said to Zebedee, 'wasn't it?'

'Anything's possible,' said Zebedee.

There was a YOO! HOO! from the other room.

Ermintrude put her head round the door.

'The kettle's on,' she said. 'Anyone for tea?'

Everyone was very glad to see Ermintrude back and also quite glad that tea was ready.

'Coming for a cup, old chumpy chops?' said Brian.

'Yes . . . er . . . in just a minute,' said Dougal. 'You go on and . . . er . . . keep me a cake.'

Everyone went into the other room for tea

and Dougal heard them asking Ermintrude what it was like to disappear, etc. . . . etc. . . .

He tiptoed across and closed the door.

'Now,' he thought, 'let's have a bit of magic. I wonder where he keeps it.'

He rummaged around in the drawers of Zebedee's desk and finally came across a little book labelled:

O.H.M.S.

DANGER – MAGIC SPELLS (MARK II)

'Aha!' thought Dougal. 'Oho!' And he looked through the book. There were various chapters headed

> 'Things out of paper-bags'
> 'Things disappearing'
> 'Things reappearing'
> 'Things exploding'

but right at the end there was a short chapter which just said,

'SECRET THINGS – NOT TO BE READ BY ANYONE'

'Oho!' thought Dougal. 'Aha!' And he started to read.

Next door everyone was enjoying tea and cakes. Dylan and Fred had come back and Ermintrude was telling them all about her disappearing act with Florence.

'It was such fun,' she said. 'Just like floating.'

'We know the feeling,' said Dylan and Fred.

Florence took another cake.

'Where's Dougal?' she said.

No one knew. It was unlike Dougal to be missing when it was tea-time.

'He said he wouldn't be a minute,' said Brian.

Zebedee looked thoughtful.

'Did he stay in *there*?' he asked.

'Yes,' said Brian.

'Oh dear,' said Zebedee.

There was a bang from the other room, then another bang and a crash. The door blew open and purple smoke billowed out.

'Oh dear,' said Zebedee again.

Everyone rushed into the other room. The smoke was very dense.

'Open a window,' shouted Mr MacHenry.

Mr Rusty opened a window, and everyone waved their hankies and flapped and blew to make the smoke disappear. When it was all gone they looked around. The room was empty. On the table was a book and on the floor Zebedee's magic wand. There was no sign of Dougal.

'Whatever can have happened?' said Florence.

They all wandered about looking for a sign of Dougal, but there was nothing.

'STOP TRAMPLING ABOUT,' said a very little voice.

'Listen!' said Brian.

Everyone listened.

'STOP TRAMPLING ABOUT!!' said the voice again.

'I know that voice,' said Brian, '– it's old shaggy! Come out, hidden friend!!'

'I AM OUT!' said the voice. 'I'M DOWN HERE!!'

Everyone looked. Under the table was a very, very small furry bundle. It was Dougal, about two inches long and looking very sad.

Brian went very close and looked at him.

'My little friend!' he said. 'Why are you so small?'

'I'VE NOT BEEN WELL,' said Dougal, sarcastically.

'Just a minute,' said Brian, 'you're not very easy to hear. Stay there!'

He got a piece of cardboard and told Florence to twist it into a trumpet shape. Then he put it close to Dougal.

'Speak now, old chum,' he said.

'DO SOMETHING!' said Dougal, so loudly that Brian fell over backwards.

'What *happened*, Dougal?' said Florence.

'I think I know what happened,' said Zebedee, sternly. 'You've been reading my book, haven't you?'

Dougal nodded miserably.

'YES!!' he bellowed through the trumpet. 'I'M SORRY!!'

'So you should be,' said Zebedee, and he winked at Florence.

'HOW LONG WILL I BE LIKE THIS?!!' asked Dougal.

'There's no need to shout, wee one,' said Ermintrude.

'Can you turn him back?' whispered Florence to Zebedee.

'Yes,' whispered Zebedee.

'Are you sorry?' he asked Dougal.

'YES!' said Dougal.

'Will you ever do it again?' asked Zebedee.

'NEVER!' said Dougal.

'Hey, you're not going to make him big again, are you?' said Brian. 'I like him like that.'

'DON'T INTERFERE!' shouted Dougal.

'But you're lovely little,' said Brian.

'You are rather,' said Florence.

'Adorable,' said Ermintrude.

'ROTTERS!' shouted Dougal, and he scuttled on to Brian, up his shell and on to his head. 'ROTTERS!'

Zebedee muttered a few words and gave a twitch of his moustache.

Dougal was suddenly his normal size again and Brian collapsed with a 'WHOOSH'.

Dougal shook himself, looked at Brian and giggled.

'Who's your flat friend?' he said to Florence.

'Dougal, you're *awful*,' said Florence.

'I know,' said Dougal. 'Any cake left?'

And, of course, there was.